1982:
A Prequel to Orwell's 1984

Malcom Massey

August 2021/ August 1982

"Thus, in setting an American agenda for a New World Order, we must begin with a profound alteration in traditional thought."

~Deceiver in Chief (DIC)
New Acirema WEFSOC

New World Order
Politics

The term "new world order" refers to a new period of history evidencing dramatic change in world political thought and the balance of power. Despite varied interpretations of this term, it is primarily associated with the ideological notion of world governance only in the sense of new collective efforts to identify, understand, or address global problems that go beyond the capacity of individual nation-states to solve.

Source: WikiMundia   August 25, 1982

Legal and Disclaimer

ISBN: 9798534703573

Library of Congress Number: Pending

Disclaimer:

Dedication and Acknowledgements

This novel is dedicated to all those who would turn back the clock to a better, safer time, and to the ones who will guide us as we are propelled forward to face a new and uncertain future.

My special thanks to two men whom I respect for their opinions and their views, two men who greatly encouraged me on this novel concept. Thank you, Mike and John.

No acknowledgement would be complete in a novel of this type without thanking the author of the original novel to which this work is offered as a prequel, not THE prequel to end all, but a close examination of one possible timeline and sequence of events. In the best tradition of fan fiction, I offer "1982: A Prequel to Orwell's 1984".

Thank you to George Orwell, author of "1984", Copyright 1949, whose original concept, work and rights I respect. I highly recommend that you read "1984" before and again after you read this short novel.

Malcom Massey

Contents

Malcom Massey

Introduction

December 21, 1983

1982 was the year everything changed. The beginning of the end. You know 1982 as 2021, under the Old Timeline.

No matter how tragic Old Timeline 2020 had been (pandemic, lockdowns, loss of freedoms, economic disaster), Old Timeline 2021 was worse, far worse. The breaking point came in 2021. That fact alone is enough to explain why the calendar has been pushed backward.

Follow with me as I take you back in time, just as the OverState has done to us in a scenario not so very far down the road. We are living a bizarre New Normal.

As I write this, the Transition Year 1982 is behind us. We survived, some of us anyway. The year is 1983, the Year of Consolidation. The specific date on the New Calendar is December 21, 1983, as I have annotated the page above.

You may ask, how can it possibly be 1983? What happened to 2021? What has brought about this bewildering change? We only have to look slightly ahead to understand this historic calendar reset. Let's walk through the changes.

2021/1982 (as the year was referred to for the first 30 days of The Transition) was a year no citizen wants to repeat, a year of intense and disruptive transformation, following months of global unrest. In every sense, 1983 has been worse still, the year of Consolidation of the events set in motion in 2021/1982. 1983 set in concrete the path that was decided for us in 1982.

Have I confused you yet? I apologize for that, but confusion is the intent of The OverState for all of us, it seems.

The OverState leverages confusion, a virtual socio-political shock and awe campaign in its fervor to erase conservative thought and with it all perceived societal ills.

This has been done to keep citizens off-kilter, walking on a tilting, ever-shifting platform. Overloading the system to its breaking point through endless, mindless actions and activities is key to maintaining OverState control.

It's as if a heavy black curtain has descended on the stage that was America, but the ropes to raise it have been jammed.

I'm eager to tell you how it began, how it all happened, how it's going. In fact, *I feel a responsibility to do so.* People like me are partly responsible for what has taken place.

I want you to know what's going on, before anything else changes, before our memories fade. There is so much to share. Some of it will confuse, amaze, bewilder, or mystify you. The global extent of the changes will astound most readers. The rage sets in when you realize that this reset has been planned in plain sight for decades. What is most amazing is that society as a whole seems accepting of the drastic change we are undergoing, as if it's normal. "It could always be worse", the saying goes. Such sheep.

I know that sharing with you in writing will not last, but I trust writing more than to just tell you. Besides, there are listening devices everywhere. The OverState always listens.

I also know that this information, presented without OverState review, is dangerous. It's as dangerous for you to read as it has been for me to write. It's illegal, actually.

So then, read quickly, with purpose. I intentionally kept this warning short, just the basics. If there were more time, I could have written volumes. Internalize these words and ponder their meaning in your particular case. Memorize portions in case your copy gets confiscated. Remember, we only hold our possessions to the next checkpoint.

At some point I fully expect this document will be censored, removed, scrubbed from existence. Then this warning account will disappear. The fact that you found it, that it has not been deleted, is an encouraging sign.

Be wise as serpents and harmless as doves, for now. Consider soberly, sift carefully, whatever is told to you from this day forward. Be discerning in what you accept or believe.

How will you know if information is false?
- Whatever is said to not be true, may very well be true
- Fact-checkers are paid propaganda, not fact sources
- Trust nothing that you cannot verify. Nothing.
- Look away from the Big Story to the Real Story
- Be suspicious in all things, complacent in none.

I hope this helps you. I hope you can use it to see what's coming, to make a plan, to be ready. 1984 will be here sooner than you think.

Tell everyone you know what you have learned from this book. Hide a copy for future reference, in paper form rather than digital, to be sure it survives all but the most final purges. Do these things now, before it's too late.

Good Luck and Godspeed.

My parting salutation to you, good reader, is a poem I recently posted to my uncle, Winston S., currently living in London. I don't know if he will ever see it. After December 31 of this year, New 1983, personal posted letters take low priority, must be submitted to the OverState authorities for screening prior to being mailed, and are subject to indefinite delivery dates.

May We Always Meet
~

To the future or the past
as the case may be
~ Greetings~
As dead men walk, walk we today
take heed you do not fail
pierce the earth
pierce the sky
pierce the obscuring veil.

~

May we always meet in the place
where there is no darkness.

Malcom Massey

Chapter 1 My Story

December 21, 1983

I realize I should get right to it. The information that I possess, the details you need to know, are that urgent.

Permit me a word about myself, as your source.

My name is Winton S. That's what it reads on my press pass and ID tag. Last names aren't used anymore, since we all have a number. My name is sort of a namesake from my Uncle Winston, except for the misspelling I received at the hands of an inept clerk in Birth Records back in Britain. The Board of Immigration in the U.S. kept it that way when I was admitted. My mother was American, my father British. She died when I was a child, my father passed more recently. I qualified for dual citizenship, which I accepted. I am an American to the core, independent and free.

I am also an independent journalist. Guilty as charged for not getting the truth into the hands of citizens soon enough. I did try, but every civilian periodical I worked for suppressed my stories and my goal of truth-telling. I still do not believe it's too late, just that our return to sanity is going to be a long slog. And that's if we start now, today.

I served 2 years in the U.S. Army Communications Corps. I might be there still were it not for a random tick-bite I received while at Ft. Eustis Virginia USA, the Army's Training and Doctrine center. The virus I contracted ended my dream.

I contracted what I term Vegan Syndrome. I break into life threatening hives at the first taste of beef or pork. *Alpha-gal* is the medical term for it. Evidence shows this disease, along with Lyme, originated at the U.S. Army Lab 257 near Long Island, hence a created virus. Such viruses are no longer considered a surprise. The upside is that I was already on a no-meat diet when the 1982 Shortages occurred. Meat disappeared from grocery shelves, as did most familiar American foods. Cheeseburgers are only a distant memory.

I reluctantly bowed out under a Medical Discharge. I'm glad I got out when I did. I learned a lot about the Army's plans against citizens that have become standard procedure. The Army is now a chief enforcement arm of the OverState, like the IRS. Unlike the IRS, the Army is more than just guns, with frequent patrolling displays of serious weaponry, including sonic crowd control, microwave weapons, the ubiquitous Seda-Tazers. Those were Army developed at Ft. Detrick, MD. All those people who said the Army would never take up arms against citizens were wrong.

I'm willing to share my experience about 1982 because there are many aspects that will serve as advance warnings for you. Few other accounts exist. Should I repeat a detail or appear to over-explain any point, please know that this serves as emphasis, not as oversight.

I'm going to apologize in advance for my penmanship. For a journalist on various local and national newspapers, my strokes should be better. I did learn cursive in elementary, to give you some idea of my age, but I haven't written by hand in so many years that quite honestly, *I'm rusty.* I've always preferred to write with a keyboard. Besides, future readers may not even be able to read cursive, so I print.

My printing is also atrocious because I'm writing at a truly odd angle, trying to shield my work while taking the 1600p government bus. I don't read any fellow riders as trouble, but the transport is packed with people. So many riders I could have missed something. No social distancing in place here.

This is the first time I've ever ridden the bus. Ever. Strictly avoided it up to now. The bus I am riding is dirty, crowded and cold. These buses are larger than your average city bus, metallic articulated whales that can only maneuver in the city since nearly all private vehicles have disappeared. In a very real sense, the buses are a metaphor, a microcosm of our failed society.

Combining all aspects of a part thrill/part horror ride at the Fair, public transport is unmatched in risk-taking. Once you make it past the terminal dogs and CriPols* , finally boarding the bus is where the fun really begins.

If you can find a seat, which I was lucky enough to do, that's a win. With my cane, I couldn't stand up for long on this rocking, swaying transport. I paid a "reservist", or *cuida asientos* if you are 2L certified, to sit down. A *cuida asientos* is a person who rides the bus all day guarding *(cuidar)* empty seats *(asientos)* in exchange for barter goods. My spot cost me two soap pods, a fortune. Gouged by a nameless kid.

Public transports are like the Wild West, with fistfights, knife attacks, drugs, sexual encounters, even the odd but occasional shootout. If someone dies, ID is scanned, the bodies disposed of in the ubiquitous bodycases waiting at every Access Stop.

A lot of contraband is sold on these public transports. To make matters worse, or wilder, the very back seats are the X-rated seats. From the sound of it, someone back there is having a bang at this very moment. I couldn't see them if I tried to look, so no description will be forthcoming.

Just ahead of those seats addicts openly use needles and pipes to dull the pain of daily life. Opium and other black-market drugs are openly hawked as if it were popcorn. The war on drugs was never meant to be won, it would seem.

Midways of the transport some try to sleep, mostly miners or plant workers on 24-hour release. At the very front, the driver sits in a windowless cage, heavily armed. The guard tends the driverless route computer that guides our way.

*CriPol: Crisis Police, armed with Seda-Tazers. Zaps suspects senseless, sedates 2 hrs. Leaves necrotic scar at needle site.

I'm sitting up close to the front with the oldest passengers, but I'm not worried about someone seeing me write. Not even the Snitches will ride these hellish vehicles.

Snitches travel in carpools of a sort, in groups, being permitted to use OverState confiscated vehicles as they go about hunting for citizen lives to ruin for credit with The OverState. Fedbois, the Snitches counterparts, prowl in packs or gangs, with the same purpose in mind.

Neither ride the buses. Probably best for all concerned.

The reason I'm on the bus tonight is that I have just turned in my car to the vehicle confiscation authorities on the south side of town. Otherwise, I wouldn't be trapped among this rabble. With all personal vehicles scheduled to be confiscated after the New Year, most have chosen to voluntarily relinquish theirs for a credit on their NBA account. NBA is Needs Based Allowance.

Another active black market has sprung up, this one in excess fuel sales. Citizens sell whatever remains in their tanks above what it takes to make it to the confiscation yard. I sold a few liters of fuel this AM. Got paid in cigarettes. I don't smoke, but I will save these among my barter stash. We all have one.

The last day of this year, December 31, 1983, is the government deadline to turn in one's vehicle. Otherwise, cars will be confiscated, and the citizen will lose any potential credit. Either way The OverState takes ownership of all vehicles by the end of the year, so I decided to cooperate.

Small consolation to know that I received a month's credit to my needs-based allowance account, or NBA. A month's credit is nothing close to the real value. *A classic 1972 Chevy Nova.* That car turned 50 years old this year, a true classic and well-maintained. I hated to say good-bye to it. The Nova was my father's first car when he emigrated to the United States.

I at least have the satisfaction of keeping the key to the anti-theft devices, including electrical and manual fuel and battery shut offs. Their mechanics will have fun trying to move that one. They were so busy today they let me park it myself. I backed all the way to the fence next to the regular soccer stadium parking area. Away from other cars, in a spot I can find again.

One furtive glance through the steamed glass of the nearest bus window reminds me I have not seen the sun in nearly eleven months. A pall lingers over the cities all day, with the incinerators working 24 hours a day even now to keep up with the dead. Twilight seems to last all day, every day.

My current assignment is to document Objector resistance in as many forms as I can find it, attend meetings, scout locations. My work (I know of no others) will be integrated into the basic programming for an AI program known as TPI, Total Presence Intelligence. More commonly the program is just called *Think Police*, a slang term which I doubt sticks.

TPI takes everything known about a person, from their birthplace and upbringing, to their social media footprint, their occupational history, any religious affiliations, political past, including such formerly private matters as voting and bank records, medical and legal proceedings, all to provide a detailed framework for anticipating the future actions and activities of the individual.

For instance, my friend was claimed to be unstable on the basis that his parents divorced and moved while he attended university, leaving him with a discrepancy on residency status that looked distinctly as if he went homeless for a time. Demerits received on TPI negatively impacted his OverState Score, limiting both his benefits as well as his privileges.

I must admit to a wide range of mixed feelings in this assignment. I do not support this level of intrusion into the personal lives of citizens. At this point my assignment is a job, an occupation that no doubt will be short-lived. I most desire to document the transformation of this nation from a consummate capitalist standard to a totalitarian utopia. At a distance of course, so as not to get caught. No trap for this rat.

My assignment, as I mentioned, is to document the story of the resistance, obviously as a method of rooting out who and where the objectors are.

For some unknown reason my reports are classified "In Arrears", having been sidelined in the edit queue. My penchant for adding ghosted text into my submissions containing the forbidden words has something to do with these reporting delays. In any event, not one of my reports, though submitted and accepted, has been read or acted on.

A man near me is coughing lightly now, under his face covering, but I am afraid he is in for a rough go. I've heard that cough before. It won't be pretty for a few weeks. I pull my face shield out long enough to douse some cinnamon into my mouth, just a pinch. A tip from my hippie vendor friend. Don't knock it. It's worked so far.

Everyone is sick, truth be told, though most try to hide it. It's our lungs. Between the virus, damnable dirty masks, and the increasing risk of pulmonary infection as the vaxxed grew weaker has made it a dirtier world. Plus no one can get in to see a doctor, following the purge by the Agency of Health. Any medical personnel that did not agree with vaxxination as a first-place priority have been relieved of duty and most have disappeared under hard to explain circumstances.

Take the last doctor I saw. It's been over a year ago, when I had Covid. I felt ok, but my lungs wheezed after running or shooting hoops. I was negative, thank God. Doc did not push the vaxx on me. Then my doctor was removed from practice, disappeared, his office shuttered, his doors officially sealed by the OverState. The bastards can do that. No one to stop them.

Back to this crowded bus. It makes jerky stops every few hundred meters it seems, disgorging far fewer people than it takes on. The bus is currently loaded well past its maximum capacity. This is the way the buses run late in the day, especially now that so many have surrendered their vehicles. There is always a bit of a scuffle going on to squeeze aboard, once the bus has slipped into the slushy curb.

Only the cold keeps people from hanging on the outside, I suppose. It's a challenge to maintain a grip on icy metal.

All buses are fully electric now, to reduce emissions, but *once-an-hour* charging of the batteries is required. This downtime spawns inevitable delays to bus schedules. Battery banks discharge faster in the sunless cold as winter sets in. Overloaded conditions also drain batteries due to the added weight. These delays are yet another example of unintended consequences that have become standard procedure in this upside-down world.

No good solution has been found for vehicle batteries once the Lithium Wars commenced in Peru, Australia and China. The USA has significant reserves, which aren't being mined due to climate standards. Thus we supply less than 2% of the world supply.

The bus will be crowded like this at least until we get to the Benefits Processing Center, where most riders will exit the bus. That is where I plan to get out as well. I need to breathe.

My BPC appointment, for whatever good a set time will do given that government appointments are never honored, is in one hour. We'll never make it at this rate. That's ok. I'm scheduled to get the ID nano-chip injection today. All ID bands expire at the end of this month. I'm not happy about it, but I've done well to avoid it for as long as I can.

Each commercial transaction such as surrendering a car has to be declared and registered at the benefits center or BPC, otherwise the ownership change will not be considered official. In addition, the former owner could retain accident liability, receive a fine against NBA credits, or be sent directly to gulag. Or all of the above.

No one wants any of those options.

The walls, ceilings and partitions of the bus are plastered with imposing, colorless posters of all sizes. Some shout health reminders to get vaxxinated, to social distance, to be tested, to inform on those citizens you have concerns about.

The majority of these tagged, ragged posters read one of the following OverState slogans and mottos:

ALL ARE ONE

FREEDOM SPAWNS SLAVERY

IS IT GOOD FOR NEW ACIREMA?

IGNORANCE SPAWNS STRENGTH

Across this last slogan, every last poster had been graffiti altered to read "VAXXINES SPAWN VARIANTS".

Other posters preach deadline prompts, such as the last date to surrender your vehicle, or deadline to get your next vaxx. Most posters broadcast the leering, crooked smile of the Deceiver in Chief. That's what I call him anyway.

DIC for short.

One side of the DIC's face is dominated by a drooping eye, a paper "medical" mask dangles from his left ear emblazoned with a muted multi-colored rainbow flag. His facial features reveal evidence of a past stroke. Garish letters beneath his wrinkled face read: "Uncle Joe Cares About You."

So much totalitarian drivel. I mentally retch reading them. Or maybe it's the odor of sweat, unwashed clothing and smoke.

The flag shown is of course the New Acirema flag, which you may have seen through The OverState broadcasts, even before these more drastic changes. An early form of this flag began being flown at USA government buildings and embassies across the globe in 2021.

The stars have been removed, partly because the flags have to be redone in any case, since Puerto Rico and Washington D.C. will become states in 1984. 52 faceless multi-hued blobs representing the various races.

The 13 background stripes remain, but are best described as a bland rainbow of faded colors, apparently of a muted design in order to no longer trigger the intolerant ones, the "liberals" who were so demanding of such changes.

There is no more official red, white and blue for our national colors. Any display of red, white and blue results in severe penalties at the hands of the CriPols. Penalties may include NBA demerits, or labor camps.

No one is imprisoned long term anymore. All prisons have been emptied and closed; sentences commuted.

Former prisoners and hardened convicted criminals now walk among us. Yes, altercations do occur when a former inmate chances upon a witness, a juror or a prosecutor with whom they have a beef. With everyone wearing masks, how they recognize their victims is a mystery, although through increased doxxing and public record searches one can find anyone almost anywhere in the world.

The resulting revenge crimes generally occur along the lines of what those inmates had been convicted of, whether it be rape, robbery, assault...you get the picture.

Not a pretty one.

Chapter 2 The Powderkeg

December 21, 1983

The background to why our nation and our world were ripe to erupt in strife and violence is simple and easy to grasp. The truth is citizens were tired of being boxed in on every side, taxed to death, worked to death and never getting a break. Their tamped-down anger and frustration festered, grew and multiplied to the point where it could not be contained.

These conditions had been building for years, but truly intensified over the last two years. Here is the short list of issues that increased the tension and the pressure:

- Forced vaxxination schemes
- Manipulated elections
- Crippling personal tax increases to provide "services"
- Historic increases in inflation and food costs
- Surging cost and limited supply of fuel and electricity
- Mandatory vaccination schemes of unapproved jabs
- Erasure of national history through re-education edict
- Erosion of Constitutional rights
- Double standards of prosecution and sentencing
- Crippled Law Enforcement efforts
- Forced lockdowns for highly survivable diseases
- Loss of jobs, businesses and occupations
- Loss of freedoms of every description
- Loss of rights i.e. free speech, assembly and religion

That these changes took place should be of no great surprise. All along the political and society elites had been telling us what to expect. They kept nothing hidden. Their message had been on full display everywhere you looked.

Books. Motion pictures. Stage plays. Music. Even conference agendas and public education curriculums became platforms of messaging and signaling future plans.

The levels to which the entertainment media stooped amounted to outright admissions of their expected outcomes. It's as if a plan had been hatched to ruin everything that the People loved about America and being American.

And that's what it was. A planned coup and revolution, right under our noses.

But We, The People didn't listen, or we did not take the threat seriously, nor did we speak up. We mistakenly believed that we were invincible, that the American way of life was too established, too entrenched in tradition to ever be lost. We thought immigrants were coming to be American, finding out only too late that they were bringing their problems with them, the very things that caused trouble in their home country. Yet we failed to see what was coming.

Even when the decisions of the new Administration left families scrounging for shortage items in the stores, paying ever higher prices for fuel, or lining up to receive our meager benefit appeasements, we did not rebel in anger. But it was building.

Even so, America kept its powder dry, so to speak, longer than most. We waited until the very last. We relied on voting, on political answers, feeling our situation was not as bad as other parts of the world. Were we too docile, too accepting of one erosion of our rights after another? After August 11, 1982 all hell broke loose. By then it was too late.

The "Days of Crisis" were not limited to the United States. Other countries were not so patient, initiating action early on. They knew better than we what was at stake.

France, a nation known for rioting, had the most severe riots in its history, in opposition to rising costs, lockdowns and vaccine mandates.

Australia, a nation completely shut down, revolted as long-haul tractor & trailer rigs blocked bridges and harbor entrances, while cargo ships effectively blocked harbors from the sea. Daily citizen-objector beatdowns are shown on TV.

Haiti rioted after it's President was assassinated, allegedly for refusing to vaccinate his people. This story was repeated across Africa. South Africa, while it did not suffer the atrocity of assassinations, nevertheless rioted against lockdown in an historic, tragic way.

Taiwan deserves the resistance trophy. After seeing Hong Kong fall under constant assault from China, Taiwan knew they were next. Taiwan resistance commandeered a U.S. Navy aircraft carrier, destroying China's existing administration buildings and air defenses in a Pearl Harbor style attack. They even had their own pilot crews. Though the attack ultimately failed, with the carrier sunk and the loss of all aboard, Taiwan's efforts gave a stark example of the distance one must go to strike a blow for freedom. May we all be up to the task, and to their example.

Closer to home Cuba erupted in historic freedom riots, which the U.S. did not assist or interfere with. Freedom was no longer a tenet of The Overstate on its rise to power.

Canada suffered severely under lockdowns, with pending elections suspended indefinitely and required vaccine passports for all. Churches were forcefully closed, their pastors arrested & jailed.

Vaxxination resistance became an issue, inflamed in the media with false statistics and claims of unvaxxinated virus transmission. In truth vaxxinated people were dying in droves, not the unvaxxinated. Double and triple vaxxinated people were dying so fast that by August 1, 2021 the current Administration in power began dropping off black bodycases, 2-meter-long vinyl cases with lids. First positioned at hospitals and morgues, then later at vaxxination centers, clinics and big box retailers. Before it was over, bodycases were being dropped at the entrance to every neighborhood like so many corpse trash cans, to be filled two to three bodies at a time and sealed. Army engineers passed by to remove the cases for incineration, often interrupting impromptu curbside funeral services in progress to stay on their collection schedule. The bodies were unceremoniously incinerated.

Finally losing their patience when the events of August 10 and 11, 2021 unfolded, Patriots fought back. They sent armed companies to state capitals, to the nation's capitol, to strategic points in every state, to harbors. They commandeered National Guard armories and unveiled their formidable arms caches. They nearly won.

Had the internet not gone down along with all other forms of personal communication, Patriots might have prevailed. This global outage was not just signaled, but directly stated by the leader of the World Economic Fund, of the INTENT and GOAL of the WEF to "cripple society as a whole through a major cyber-attack".

With only Ham radio, CB's and walkie-talkies to plan and strategize, the Patriots did not last long, especially once military air strikes were called in. Their crushed and burned vehicles, their torched and strafed homes have not been permitted to be moved, razed or repaired, leaving vivid reminders on every corner of the penalty for insurrection under the harsh reality that is The OverState.

Labelled "Objectors" for their role in denying the official results of the previous election and "Plague Rats" for their resistance to mandated vaxxinations, Patriot objectors were literally hunted.

The ones with a food supply set aside, with weapons and ammunition to guard themselves, and a dependable water supply, the Objectors wanted nothing more than to be left alone, to live in peace and pursue their own lives.

Painted by the media as selfish racists, or ratted out by Snitches and Fedbois, most Objectors left the cities when things got bad, or already lived outside the population centers. Eventually their vehicles were confiscated, their electricity shut off, their ability to buy & sell eliminated. Some fought and died valiantly.

Most surrendered, hoping for unfound leniency. Objectors who make the OverState's Blacklist are stripped of citizenship, are sent to re-education camps and gulag, and become prison labor in service to the OverState.

Refusal of any vaxx, any Patriotic speech or display, or any report by a Snitch or Fedboi of such activity, verified or not, will land you on the Blacklist. Most ended up there through voting records and results of the door-to-door vaxx sweep conducted in 1982. Yes, they did make a list.

The unintended consequence of this situation is that most Objectors were also those Americans with the greatest knowledge and contribution to putting food on American tables. With the majority of them jailed or in hiding, farming has collapsed, thus drastically limiting food supply and quality. Now any food they produce they keep for themselves.

Pockets of resistance are still rumored to exist. Part of my assignment is to find these pockets, infiltrate them, and report back. I have been successful on the first two points. I have yet to submit a useful report, but that is for your ears only.

I will tell you this much.

I have verified the existence of 800 facilities, vacant up to now, that were built by FEMA over the last two decades which can house up to 10,000 "residents" at a time. These bear all the hallmarks of a POW camp, fences, guard towers, the works.

These camps are consistently located at the end of rural rail spurs and appear to have no current industrial use. Each camp has large incinerators with capacities greatly exceeding the amount of garbage that could be produced even if populated beyond capacity.

Add to that my confirmation of 102,000 confirmed boxcars that have been obtained under FEMA's budget, complete with shackles. Or 30,000 *guillotines*. Under FEMA. Do they operate under some French revolution delusion? What Emergency is being strategized to be Managed by Federal Authorities?

In reality, I do not know what these facts mean. Perhaps nothing, if taken separately. Summed together, I feel that plans are being made for some segment of our population that are not on the up and up.

One more thing. I am not the only person who is aware of these details.

Now you are also aware.

Chapter 3 The Spark

> *"Beware of driving men to desperation...*
> *a cornered rat is dangerous".*
> ~*Winston Churchill*

December 21, 1983

What was the spark, you ask? What lit the fuse on this powderkeg of violent, unpopular sentiment?

The virus and imposed pandemic were just tinder to the firestorm that erupted in August 2021.

The spark came down to the highly disputed 2020 election. Not that the societal and political changes I have described have not been years in the planning by The OverState. They have. We see that now.

But by August 10, 2021 when the side currently in power realized their massive election fraud had been discovered and proven, they put their years-long set of plans into action.

The fraudulently installed President, the one I call Deceiver in Chief, the DIC for New Acirema, set the stage by stating publicly that the "Days of Crisis" in America were the worst since the Civil War. Imagine. *The Civil War* with all its horror, atrocities, loss of life, aggression and pain. The war that used slavery as an excuse to exercise dominance and control. These are words he spoke, hyperbole to light the fuse of this new American revolution.

The DIC went on to say that January 6, when Objectors marched on the U.S. Capitol, was worse than 9/11. No matter what our politics may be, there is no logical comparison between these two events, 9/11 being the worst of the two, IMO. These inflammatory words were prefaced, I might add, by prior DIC speeches taunting Patriots that they were up against nuclear weapons should they attempt to challenge the installed and acting government. As if to emphasize the control they hold, torture of January 6 detainees was revealed.

The OverState quickly moved to seize control of all power in Washington D.C., (which happens to be our 51ˢᵗ state by the way).

Because their flagrant election fraud was uncovered. Because they felt threatened. Because they were losing control.

Permit me to spell out the whole two-week timeline here for you:

August 10, 2021
- Voting Fraud Proven in Four U.S. States, reversing the 2020 Presidential Election. Congress recalls delegates
- Deceiver in Chief declares 10 Days of Crisis for America, essentially a State of Emergency.
- DIC suspends 2ⁿᵈ Amendment rights. No weapon is to be displayed in public.
- Public riots begin locally with Objector calls to march on Washington. VA, MD National guard called up.

August 11, 2021
- Scheduled Joint FCC & FEMA Nationwide Emergency Alert System test. Made joint w/UK and Australia. Included both radio and wifi warning systems. Test "goes awry", radio broadcast and wireless internet connections blocked; global communications outage.
- Military leaders quietly purged and held on base arrest.
- Congress disbanded but restricted to their respective House and Senate buildings to control information.
- Mass riots and looting ensue. 1982 Hoarding Shortage
- National Guard and U.S. Army called up to block highways, defend Washington, D.C. "OP Ring of Fire"
- Deadly force authorized by DIC. Battle of 1982 begins.
- HAARP weather system unleashed to produce rain & floods across U.S., incapacitating ground travel.

August 25, 2021/1982

- OverState Established, name used for first time. U.S. Constitution and Bill of Rights suspended.
- Executive Orders 001 thru 010 NEOs signed/enacted
- Calendar Year 2021 reset to 1982 by NEO – 001
- Transitional Period declared for the balance of 1982.
- All 2nd Amendment rights declared null and void.
- Weapons confiscation begins under penalty of death.
- All Churches Shuttered, Doors Blocked or Welded Shut
- All gatherings forbidden, of any description or purpose
- All Fossil fuels (gas, oil, coal) nationalized & shuttered.
- Newspapers nationalized. All Journalists conscripted.
- Grocery retailers & distribution networks nationalized.
- 2022 Reset to 1983 -The Year of Consolidation
- January 1, 2023 Reset to January 1, 1984.

Strategically, all bases were covered. The OverState had set the stage. Now the business of putting plans into action began. It was not pretty, for months, the Battle of 1982, the Operation Ring of Fire around Washington, D.C. The 1982 Shortages and Hoarding were the worst, when people realized there would be no restocking of stores on any regular or normal basis. Panic set in, turning neighbor against neighbor, friend against friend.

I won't go into detail here. Another time perhaps. I'll try not to overwhelm you with all that we have been through.

Chapter 4 The Present Situation

December 21, 1983

Pulling my damp balaclava away from my mouth long enough to take a sip, I ponder my work so far. My metal canteen canister clinks against my pencil as I look around the cavernous bus. Something, or someone, stinks.

My stark observation is that not one person aboard was prepared for the range of changes that have occurred. None of us, not even myself. Which I find strange, that I was not prepared, serving as I did 2 years in the Army, and then being raised by a "prepper" as my father was called. I failed miserably. I did not have enough food, enough water to go into the Transition with any sense of preparedness or security.

I had no weapons other than a few knives. "Adapt, improvise, survive" became my bywords. I've learned to scrounge with the best of them. I am basically homeless, losing the last regular bed I've slept in over a year ago, since the London tragedy.

I have friends who have put me up from time to time, but I truly hate to impose. There always seems to be a catch. I do not know where I will sleep tonight.

Without a kitchen, I rarely cook. The feeding lines on every corner are 1) too long 2) hot-beds of solicitation and pilferage. I can't afford to lose time or money.

The green protein I am drinking at present is a substitute food I bartertrade from a vendor I regularly see on the streets. I prefer the powder form, because water is free and surprisingly plentiful, one of the few utilities that works. Many citizens have questions and concerns about the water quality and content. They say the OverState adds chemicals such as fluoride and THM to keep citizens dumb and docile, THMs being the worst of the two. My research says they are correct.

THMs are tri-halomethanes, by-products of water purification by certain chlorine compounds in conjunction with high organic loads.

THMs are known to increase cancer, neurological and miscarriage risks as far back as 1976, according to one U.S. Army study. THMs increase with the high particulate, low initial water quality.

I have never tested the water I most often drink. My main source for weeks has been an old playground water fountain I found in a neglected riverside park. The fountain is fed from a spring in the side of the cliff if the engraved placard can be believed. The older pipes probably add a healthy dose of copper and lead, but I'm trusting those elements to kill off any disease the water may contain.

Kind of a hippie chick, Mara, my protein vendor is one of a hundred street vendors that operate unchecked in the city. She small batch creates the protein powder I mix in my water canister. Mara also turns out great protein bars of which I am a *huge* fan. So far, she has managed to find grains and syrups for her unbaked creations from shuttered shops.

Mara always smells like plants and flowers, which is odd because I never see plants and flowers anymore. All outdoor plants in the city have died under the pall and haze that covers us. Mara says all her ingredients are natural, all grown organically in her secret garden below the city. I take that to mean a basement somewhere nearby, but I don't really know. Wartime London grew food gardens below city streets in WWII.

I also bought salve Mara made up that healed my bruises, my cuts *and my pain* from injuries I suffered during a robbery attempt (I somehow survived). That's how I ended up with this cane. Held onto my pack but gained a limp. The blend smelled greatly of lavender and pine, but it alleviated my symptoms, the thing I needed most. No one can afford any downtime these days.

Survival is a constant scramble, a daily race. Except that now I can't run it like I used to.

I glance forward out the frosted window. Dusk is falling. The buildings, streetlights, signs are in such disrepair.

The bus lurches right and slides to the curb. The door opens, the stiff breeze pelting pellets of sleet through the space.

No one appears, then a ragged Wildman jumps on just before the door closes. His clothes are tattered, his eyes crazed, his neck scarred with dozens of Seda-Tazer marks. I try to look away, but we have made eye contact. I close my notepad, clamping my pen inside. He stares through me, punching his fists together rapidly, a challenge for my seat. I grip my cane tighter in my gloved right hand. I prepare to stand when the entire front of the bus, the ceiling above and all forward windows blaze with a pulsing strobe of blue-white light. I glance down to avoid the flash, knowing what to expect, averting eyes just long enough.

The door of the bus bursts open under the force of heavy truncheons, followed by the black fur blitz of a pair of CriPol hounds.

The Wildman turns away from me as the hounds' snarling mouths snap onto his wrists, pulling his hands away from his throat. The horrid crackle of the Seda-Tazer sings its song, landing a tazer dart in the Wildman's neck, just above his Adam's apple. The dogs release at the right moment to avoid being shocked, allowing the man's body to hit the floor soundly. The writhing lasts only moments before the sedative takes over. Makes a man sleep a minimum of 2 hours.

I know only a little about the sedative. Considered humane, it is called Silk and is made from opium. Assisted suicide, the new OverState initiative called SSP, uses a stronger version of the same drug.

As the CriPols drag the body down the steps and through a trace of snow, the crowd on the bus starts to chant, stomping their feet to show their impatience. Again, I look down.

I can hear the footsteps as the TPI counselor boards. Think Police. The crowd is always surveyed after an incident to see if any related individuals need to be "interviewed". Think Police are exclusively female, are abnormally inquisitive and frankly intimidating. It is their training.

I pretend to be asleep. Soon the footsteps retreat, the door closes. The bus grinds gears and growls away from the curb. The chants stop and everyone goes back to whatever they were doing before. It is as if nothing happened, commonplace.

This astounds me. But what amazes me even more is that most citizens don't seem to realize how bad our lot truly is, that we have been taken over, a Revolution, a *Coup D'état*. They buy the line that all this disruption is for their good, for "safety", for our "democracy". They can't see the forest for the trees. All holidays have now been cancelled. No public *or private* celebrations are to be held that are connected with America's founding, nor with any religion or other affiliation.

Most of my fellow riders are "ostriched", as the new insult goes, heads in the sand, mindlessly preparing for Christmas with little on the table and less in the way of gifts to exchange. They prattle on to each other about when life will get back to normal, how the next election cycle will bring corrections, about when the past President (we dare not speak his name) will re-assert his power.

All that is gone, finished, over in my book. I can't look back. I want to grab their lapels and shake them into consciousness. Of course, I dare not even bring up the topic.

With ongoing pandemic pronouncements, citizens are brutally discouraged from gathering in groups, or completely prohibited in some regions of OverState strength. How would they ever communicate to re-organize? All political options are off the table regardless. Plus Uncle Joe is always listening.

There no longer exists any right to vote. No candidate stands to be voted for. Traditional political solutions are out.

No personal communication technology exists, other that our ID chip or bracelet. The OverState blocked all cell phones.

Most believe the balance of Power was tipped toward this slippery evil slope with the introduction of a bill in the US Senate on August 10th, 2021, threatening decertification of the election results of 4 states. If advanced, this would have changed enough state results to reverse the recent presidential election.

As I have alluded to, following the Internet Blackout in the summer of 2021/1982, when the ten sweeping Executive Orders were issued, every single facet of American life changed, beginning with the calendar itself.

By August 25th of that year, the year was rolled back 1982 again, changed by Presidential decree. Circled back you might say. Congress did not vote on the decertification because they had been summarily disbanded on August 11.

The changes, and they were many, did not end with the calendar. They did not end at political, or socio-economic change. Basically, the change has never stopped, period.

I have an entire chapter for you on the Ten Executive Orders. You're going to be amazed at what has taken place. Just not in a good way.

Try not to be too harsh on yourself for not seeing this coming down the pike. We all labored behind a veil prior to these apocalyptic revelations.

It is my hope that we may achieve a synergistic energy that will propel us forward through our darkest days, so that we may come out on the other side of this nightmare with some semblance of liberty and freedom.

We may not be able to see it now. Right now it is difficult to see the forest for the trees. But if we keep looking for the light, the revelations, the cracks in the OverState system that permit us to chip away at their iron grip, we may succeed.

The men who won the American Revolution against my British ancestors were often hungry, shoeless, poorly dressed for the winter weather in which they fought. They were in want of shot, of powder, of cannon. Yet they prevailed.

So shall we.

Chapter 5 Winston S.

"At this moment, for example, in 1984 (if it was 1984)..."
~Winston S., 1984

December 21, 1983

Before we get to the Ten NEOs, I want to introduce you to a very important person. My Uncle Winston. Some of you have already heard of him. He was a prominent British print journalist and still lives in London, as far as I know. I have always believed he was destined for importance. Not fame necessarily, just the accomplished greatness of the person ahead of their own time.

Uncle Winston has acted as my main source of inspiration and information, both before and after I became a journalist, even before my father passed. Winston is insightful and canny. We have communicated over the years by traditional mail post. Winston does not have a telephone. A book lover, he assisted in a second-hand bookstore for a time, he also loves film, older stuff, with real stars and music.

Winston is currently assigned to the Global Agency of Truth in London. Personally speaking, he was writing a new book as of the last time we corresponded, though when or if that work will be published is unknown. The title, likely to be a date, is equally uncertain.

Winston refers to himself as a "smith" by occupation, as in word-smith. Being of the old school of journalism, he likes the term; says it implies skilled work. To be known as a word-smith is a compliment as far as he is concerned. He refers to all his colleagues, those that remain, as his fellow "smiths". DoubleSpeak is their language, their tool in trade.

The Agency of Truth – New Acirema District, where I work and receive my assignments, is like all named Agencies of The OverState government, subject to name change amid final reorganization come January 1, 1984.

That is the official end of the Consolidation phase of this new world order. Globally, WEFCOM is voting on it this week, though results will take longer to be shaped and molded by the Technocratic branch of government before being publicly revealed, which covers the Agency of History and the Agency of Truth.

As of that time, Uncle Winston will be reassigned from the Agency of Truth to whatever more permanent form is decided once 1984 arrives. Keen on their Agency designations, some at WEFCOM contend vehemently for the term Ministry, if you can believe the nightly broadcasts. In any case, in a few days, all will be known and made clear and final.

The Agency of Truth, hurriedly formed in August of 1982, appeared overnight, created to protect The OverState and the general public against the continued onslaught of purportedly false information being disseminated regarding election challenges, medical science opposition and an onslaught of conspiratorial thinking in print, online and over the airwaves.

Created in a tantrum-type reaction to joyous overflowing Patriotism on display July 4th, 2021, a batch of ten Executive Orders was hastily drafted the night of July 5th, now termed NEO's. Every socialist-globalist representative and Senator, combined with several independents and some conservatives, wrote out their totalitarian dream list, consumed with embarrassment at the riotous Independence Day celebrations across the USA. Those in power felt threatened and triggered. Enough was enough.

Most citizens were watching or blasting fireworks, cooking out and celebrating, unaware of the machinations that would likely cause this to be the last true Independence Day celebration for the rest of their lives.

A small news release mentioned Congress working into the night on some urgent matters, but corporate media did not carry the news. Essentially no one paid much attention, a recurring error made by liberty lovers.

Neither the existence nor extent of these Executive Orders was revealed until the internet came back online the night of August 25, 2021, or more correctly, *August 25, 1982*, when the orders were signed into law for immediate enactment.

On this date, we were made aware of this batch of life-changing, game-changing Executive Orders issued by the Deceiver in Chief, as he is called, though not in a voice above a whisper and never within range of an electronic device.

Per NEO 002, all print and video journalists became conscripted workers in the New Language Centers at the Agency of Truth. Former newspaper publishing buildings were repurposed to house these workers as well as their required writing equipment. After their initial conscription obligation, journalists or word-smiths, will be permitted to live in alternate dormitory- style housing for a 24-hour release. They are sequestered like juries to control information flow.

The computer monitors and processors of the word-smiths are ancient, from what I've seen, but by virtue of their limited capacity are immune to hacking and sufficient to the task before them. Rewriting history, writing out and erasing from memory those objectionable characters and incidents that would undermine the OverState is a despicable display of totalitarianism, but it is not the worst that we have seen.

As an independent writer under the Agency of History, I have so far escaped long-term conscription, at a time when all writers are being drafted into the service of the OverState. Many writers have disappeared after attending the journalist re-education camps. These apparently have been swallowed up in the gargantuan political maze of The OverState. My travel permit and ID, (Vaxxpass) for my current assignment are approved by the Agency of History, necessary even within the city to document my comings and goings. Employers issue such documents now.

I'm not sure how old Uncle Winston is. I've only seen him twice that I recall, once when we visited England and once when he came to the USA to see us. Though less than 50, Winston seems much older. He has seen a lot. Life has not been very kind to him. Life has taken its toll. You can read it in his longhand scrawl, his wording, his outlook.

The early loss of his parents, the OverState's involvement and subsequent estrangement of his sons, the tragic loss of his brother in the riotous days following Hate Night, the untimely death of his first wife due to the Enhanced Vaxxination Program have left the weight of time heavily upon his shoulders. I do not know if he re-married.

The enhanced part precipitated her death meaning "forced", as in door-to-door enforcement. Except that she never took the vaxxination, although many have taken it, and have been sickened and have died as a result.

Excusing herself to go to the bathroom prior to receiving the vaxx, Auntie found Uncle Winston's pistol and ended her life. She was a principled woman, true to her ideals, who chose not to live if living meant compromising to the socialistic ideals of The OverState.

As a younger member-citizen of The OverState, I have not had to receive the vaxx, yet. I joined to fly below their radar and obtain an inside track to their plans. I have a digital vaxxpass card marked "Co-Op" and a medical waiver override due to contracting C19 itself early in the First Pandemic. The Vegan Syndrome, a tick-vector illness, precludes me from and injection of animal proteins. The vaxx contains SM-102.

Not having the vaxx, which is evident by metal detecting scanner, gives me the cover I need to uncover the objector resistance. Otherwise, I would not be welcome among them.

More than one time I have been taken to their camps for training, mostly with firearms. Until now I have passed muster. I trust that will continue.

I have not told Winston about my journalistic assignment. I do know that he favors gun ownership, having seen a duck gun over his fireplace mantel, just like my father's at the farm.

Uncle Winston's burdened sense of optimism encouraged me to be a writer. With the advent of online publishing, he foresaw a brighter light, a new opportunity for writers, to be independent in their writing, their publishing, their careers. Former ways of publishing had always been traditional, limited and forced. Limitations were imposed, some by publishers, some by the authors themselves, to make published authorship a very exclusive club.

Some independent journalists, myself included, were briefly able to parlay this short-lived freedom into a source of income. I have several books published, pure escapism adventures, others self-help books. Together these bring a tidy sum of credits each month, though word is our copyrights will be taken away at the end of this year. All books are considered a threat to the OverState. Creative minds are not valued, nor is creativity encouraged. Compliance is the name of the game, one's saving grace, the gold behavior standard.

Darkened movie houses and theaters, once Winston's favorite pastime, have been repurposed to OverState education centers, their screens flickering with dull black and white images of speakers droning on from mind-numbing scripts. Viewership is paid instantly in NBA credits.

Movies shown "re-educate" the public on matters ranging from gender propaganda to vaxxine "science" to the new OverState's political neutrality push. Theater stages employ former crisis actors to portray "re-education nights", acting out tenets of the CRT program, now simply known as Our History.

Shopping malls have been closed, re-opening only after extensive renovation and the removal of all private signage to become OverState centers for issuing rations, receiving "services" and of course detention.

Larger retailers were pressured by the OverState early on into initiating payment "coordination" plans whereby one's vaxx status and OverState Score was connected to their NBA account. Be a good citizen, take the vaxx, buy more goods.

Low OverState Scores require an intervention appointment with a behavioral counselor, like a probation officer, with citizens warned of their precarious social status.

Neither checks, bank cards, nor phone apps are valid banking instruments any longer. This is the one change people did see coming, having been warned about it multiple times.

Prophetic verses from the Revelation to St. John have long been quoted regarding the future of having to receive a mark in the hand or forehead to be able to buy and sell. This one came true just as written, the "Mark of the Beast".

When all cash was declared worthless paper in August 1982, an economic crash of epic proportions occurred. The OverState instantly provided a ready-made solution, as if they had planned it all along. We were immediately "offered" a nano-chip injected into our hand, between the thumb and forefinger, digitally connected to our NBA accounts and ID. Those who accepted received a monthly Needs Based Allowance. All who refused were left to barter, to their wits.

If medically restricted, such as myself, a permanent rubberized wrist band was permitted to be worn. I requested this method to avoid an episode of anaphylaxis from the injection. I will have to have the nano-chip implant no later than December 31, 1983, no exception. Ten days. If I do react, that is of no concern to the OverState. They bear no liability.

Even the band gives me hives in extreme heat. The skin beneath the ID band is starting to itch even as I write this.

The atmosphere on this bus is thick, and too warm for my clothes. I layered for the weather outside, not knowing how long the bus would take to arrive, or how long this ride would take. I realize that I am hungry again.

What I need most is a shower. Little chance of that today.

Chapter 6 The Ten NEOs

December 21, 1983

Published well over a year ago, the Ten New Executive Orders (NEOs) read like the OverState's Ten Commandments. The Digital Book is where they are compiled, though it is not an actual book. It is a detailed record of the damage done to America with ten strokes of the DIC's pen.

The Ten NEO's are read aloud every evening by the faceless "news" broadcast. TV personalities no longer exist. Body positivity concerns, and the message sent to Acirema's many obese residents by fit, attractive people ended that.

As the digital voice reads the Ten Neo's, it is intended that citizens drop what they are doing to read along. Compliance is digitally enforced by our screens which listen to us 24/7.

Every tribute paying citizen had to accept the Ten NEOs to receive NBA. That's the Needs Based Allowance. We received copies at the Benefits Compliance Center.

Copies were costly, nearly a full month's allowance, deducted from your NBA and downloaded to your chip or ID band. No print copies were provided or permitted.

So here they are, the Ten New Executive Orders, in order signed on August 25th, 2021/1982. All are on track to be fully enacted by the 9th Three-Year-Plan starting January 1, 1984.

NEO – 001 Agency of History

Primary Impact: The New Calendar Year
- Elimination of Burden of Past Time; Rewrites History
- Forces the 2021 calendar back to 1982
- "Who Controls History Controls Destiny"

NEO – 002 Agency of Truth

Primary Impact: Rewriting of All Documents Begins

- New Language established, all public interactions
- New Dictionary created/words eliminated
- All incidents, dates, names unfavorable to The OverState to be removed ASAP.
- Starts with DoubleSpeak (NEWS) Archives.
- "Who Controls the Truth Controls History"

NEO – 003   Agency of Crime

Primary Impact: All Criminals Released, Except Political
- All sentences commuted, except political.
- All jails closed to be repurposed.
- TPI – Total Presence Intelligence - Think Police established, data matrix projects future behavior

NEO – 004   Agency of Religion

Primary Impact: Organized Religion dissolved.
- Elimination of Religious Hate Speech
- No state religion to be established.
- Public and Private Worship prohibited.
- All public religious symbols removed from public view include from churches/mosques
- No weddings permitted.

NEO – 005   Agency of Finance

Primary Impact: Cashless Society Imposed
- Digital currency/Economy created
- Elimination of All Cash & All Debt
- All banks are nationalized under The OverState
- Gov't/Student loans paid by conscripted servitude. Military and CriPol volunteers exempted
- Stock Exchange, Federal Reserve Closed
- IRS repurposed to OverState enforcement

- All tax returns eliminated
- Needs Benefit Allowance (NBA) Established Universal income established. Govt. ID required.
- NBA infraction penalty fines enacted
- All businesses nationalized, all profits and resources confiscated. Businesses continue to operate, receive monthly NBA credit to buy goods, pay staff, utilities
- Tribute becomes New term for taxes. One monthly fixed payment taken from NBA allowance. Tribute covers all granted permissions

NEO – 006   Agency of Population

Primary Impact: Depopulation Goals
- Depopulation goals made public including:
- 50% reduction is "stated" goal
- Natural Attrition insufficient for goal
- All deaths rewarded by NBA award to heirs
- SSP - Self Suicide Protocol - Guided OverState assistance available with ID.

NEO – 007   Agency of Medicine

Primary Impact: Forced Vaxxinations
- Enhanced Vaxx Protocol initiated. EVP. Monthly Citizen Vaxxinations– 8 Vaxxes Total
- Required to access NBA and privileges
- Medical appointments become an earned privilege

NEO – 008   Agency of Politics

Primary Impact: One Party System ANGSOC
- Elections Suspended
- All political parties dissolved, their leaders jailed and records confiscated.

- Legislative Branch of Government dissolved. OverState authorized branches add Technocratic to Executive & Judicial.

NEO – 009 Agency of Climate

Primary Impact: Fossil Fuels Banned
- Gas stations closed; Terminals blockaded.
- All petroleum facilities and refineries closed. All pipelines shut down.
- Coal mines remain open Exported to China
- HAARP authorized to use wifi bandwidth

NEO – 010 The New Nation

Primary Impact – America renamed New Acirema
- New flag declared no red, white & blue
- Display of red, white & blue strictly illegal
- Words Patriotism/Patriot banned
- Creation of the OverState, admitting the existence of the dual-party Deep State

Chapter 7 The Great Reset

"The only thing Orwell got wrong was the year."

~Lauren Boebert

December 21, 1983

Once the Ten NEOs were issued on August 25, 1982, The Great Reset was primed for action and set in motion. The secret plan was no longer a secret.

America was no more, falling under the auspices and rule of the World Economic Forum. The Great Reset will be complete, all boxes checked, when 1984 arrives in only 10 short days. Few hours remain in the current day.

The literal reset of our calendars from 2021 to 1982 was unnerving, to all but elements of the Deep State. The dual-party Deep State instantly became the OverState, a tacit admission of conspiracy theories dating back decades.

The OverState is neither Republican nor Democrat in their loyalties, but globalist. WEFCOM First. Elite statesmen with industry ties and huge financial stakes in old industry like steel, rail, finance, real estate and agriculture gradually admitted industries such as pharmacology and technology.

The calendar reset rolled the nation back to the year The OverState felt they had last been in solid control of the socio-political narrative. The globalist advances of the Deep State began to take hold in the early 1980s, then suffered a setback under Reagan. An unrelenting cascade of ultra-progressive master plans, known as the Three-Year Plans, was initiated. This resulted in back-to-back Bill Clinton victories, as well as the Bush presidencies, both known Deep State members.

Starting with a formal, focused effort as the decade of the 1990s began, elite globalists commenced meeting annually, specifically to plan the demise of free society.

36

Finding the UN cumbersome, new globalist groups spawned from such global gatherings as NATO and the G-7 economy conference, the Davos and Bilderberg groups formed.

Choosing to not meet in America, all globalist groups preferred elite meeting sites across Europe; London, Geneva, Berlin. All members of the OverState are also simultaneously included in the Davos Summit, the Bilderberg Group, G-7, as well as becoming life members of the World Economic Forum.

Each participating nation at Davos and Bilderberg was tasked with creating its own Three-Year Plan.

While the Great Reset is a globalist concept and is the primary goal of each successive Three-Year Plan, the concept of set-year plans specifically came from China. China learned to maintain complete control over its people following the Great Communist Revolution of 1949 by using well executed set-year plans. Thus, the Three-Year Plans are inspired by China's system of multi-year plans to maintain political grip.

The three year interval forces planning well in advance of each subsequent Political Cycle. Every three years a globalist goal was set, enacted to advance their great utopia, and rewritten once accomplished. They focused and they won.

Written in excruciating detail and approved by the Deep State, the 1st *American* Three-Year Plan was originally put into action in 1998. Every three years after, another plan was written containing the following topics:

- Climate Control
- Peace and Armament
- Global Health & Population Control
- World Economics
- (NEWS) Narrative Enactment - Warranted Syncopation

Three-Year Plans set in motion political, financial and social change that accomplished the goals of the OverState through a series of strategic but persistent small steps.

Every three years since, the plan has been modified and updated to achieve more of their goals.

It's like the old saw of how to eat an elephant. That's how they brought America to its knees, one bite at a time.

What actually has been reset? Far more than you may imagine, more than our calendar. A great many other areas have been reset as well.

As we approach 1984, we enter the 9th Three-Year Plan to be specific. This will be the Year of greatest suffering.

You may wonder why.

It's all in the Book of the Ten NEOs. We are faced with a chilling, heartless scenario. The scramble to survive is on.

Our population has been culled by nearly half, a combination of starvation, vaccine-related deaths, and disease.

Acirema does not know how it will feed itself, how it will clothe itself, if they will even survive whatever happens next.

Trust Uncle Joe, the posters say. Uncle Joe cares like a brother, say others. A big bully of a brother, in my book.

Our political system has ceased to exist. Congress has been disbanded, permanently. With the Constitution and Bill of Rights suspended indefinitely, many feel our society will never again be guided by these documents.

This means:

- No votes will ever again be cast
- No individual rights or freedoms exist
- Digital intrusion into everything we do
- No individual property ownership.
- All worship of God or gods eliminated

Debates rage about who the lucky ones are, the survivors or the ones who succumbed to the madness and the destruction.

With America now on her knees, hands behind her back, the executioner sharpens his axe, awaiting the final proclamation. Who will save her?

Chapter 8 The Agency of Truth

"The further a society drifts from the truth,
The more it will hate those that speak it."
~*George Orwell*

December 21, 1983

With the creation of The Agency of Truth, few things have consumed more labor than the complete deconstruction and reconstruction of what is officially considered true and false. Thousands of writers and journalists work day and night to rewrite every document written in this nation's 245-years.

The *New Dictionary* is one of the most frightening tasks undertaken by The Agency of Truth. Our very language usage is being changed. Any variance from the latest edict can result in penalties. Words have been removed, while others were added. Words have been altered or assigned a different meaning.

How was this accomplished? By copyrighting the words and terms they chose to outlaw, then pulling those terms from public use. All published or private documents have to be submitted to the Agency for Truth and will all eventually be scanned, flagged and have any illegal words or terms changed or removed. Repeat offenders are fined or sent to gulag.

In particular no political slogans are permitted, nor quotes from their candidates. For example, "Make America Great Again" and "MAGA" having been branded as hate-inciting epithets, were reworded to a bland "Permit Acirema to Exist" or "PATE" for short. No one likes it, but we recite it when instructed to do so. The phrase appeared on billboards across the country overnight, supposedly hung by Objector gulag labor from those awaiting trial for subversive activities. No one has confirmed these stories other than myself. They will not be heard on The OverState broadcast "The NWO Report".

All citizens are expected to watch "The NWO Report" at 2000p for 30 minutes. It just comes on by itself. Most public screens watch you. Soon all screens public and private will have that capability.

Following "The NWO Report" citizens then have 30 minutes to deal with necessities before the power is shut down at final curfew.

Chapter 9 The Politization of The Virus

December 21, 1983

The most controversial aspect to the 1982 takeover has been the political manipulation of the C19 virus and the associated vaxxine attempts to rectify it. All this led to the Vaxxine Wars. Allow me to update with what we now know:
The C19 Virus is known to have been:

- Generated in a laboratory
- Lab manipulated in the U.S., Canada & China
- Released from Wuhan
- A bioterrorism tool
- Created for intentional release
- Circulated world-wide

Criminal politicians lost no time seizing the crisis to lock down entire nations and populations at little risk of contracting or dying from the virus, while exposing weaker populations (the aged & the infirm) to its full range of terrors.

Under NEO – 007 the Agency of Medicine introduced EVP. Enhanced Vaxx Protocol became the global standard, a monthly total of 8 forced vaxxes simultaneously for every adult with a government ID. This is a requirement to access one's NBA allowance and associated privileges. If you do not come to the Vaxx Centers, personnel will fan out into the neighborhoods to identify and vaxx those holdouts.

Where all of this gets tricky is when the true agenda of the Agency of Medicine was revealed in conjunction with that of the Agency of Population. Two sides of the same coin.

NEO – 006 created the Agency of Population. The primary impact of this NEO was *depopulation*. Depopulation goals were made public including:

- 50% population reduction as stated goal
- Natural Attrition insufficient for stated goal

- Volunteers were welcomed through SSP - Self Suicide Protocol - Guided OverState assistance available with ID. Tens of thousands accepted.
- All new deaths result in NBA credit to heirs

The goal of Population Control, or PopCon, would be achieved when the goals of Medicine were met. When EVP was fully enacted, true PopCon goals would be maintained. The PopCon goal of 50% population reduction has been reached, or soon will be. That's 150 million people.

For the first time weeding out undesirable or unsustainable humans became an open reality, in the same way Eugenics always has been a component of abortion policy. Now the target of such policy became adult humans.

Eugenics as envisioned by Margaret Sanger inspired both Adolf Hitler's Holocaust mass murder as well as that of Planned Parenthood, who until recently featured Sanger on their web page as a founding influence. Woodrow Wilson admired Sanger's work along with her racist description of "human weeds".

There is even a movement now afoot among ANGSOC members to rename the National Institute of Health in Margaret Sanger's honor, with a plaque citing Hitler's contribution to PopCon.

Population Control in the former USA has also been revealed to have been underway since the early days of World War I, the early 1900s. Eugenics has always been a main component of PopCon.

Various PopCon proponents have risen, mostly from elite circles who felt entitled to decide who was acceptable for society and who deserved elimination. We find PopCon evidence in the deployment of toxic gases in WWI, of mass-produced petroleum-based medicines abetting the cancer epidemic, of abortions offered ever more freely to certain population groups.

We even find population control tenets forming the basic mission statements of foundations intended to impact Global Health and funded by billionaire philanthropists and would-be doctors, though these are far from Hippocrates' ideals.

Finally, in a maddening episode of contrary thinking, the more people that died in New Acirema made way for more illegal immigrants.

The Tuberculosis Crisis of late 1982 proved that unrestricted global immigration, long feared to have a negative impact on the spread of disease, resulted in a TB epidemic that threatens to decimate our most overcrowded cities. TB has spread uncontrolled and at a pace previously unseen. The vaxx left recipients with impaired immunity, unable to fight TB off. There is no vaxx or cure for TB.

The OverState's wholesale immigration policies affected medicine policy, creating a destabilizing effect through large, unhealthy populations resettled into struggling communities across Acirema. This is but one of a series of destructive acts by The OverState intentionally exposing Acirema citizens to new diseases, increasing the body count exponentially.

We knew The OverState did not have our best interests at heart. Little did we know what murderous intent they had for the unsuspecting populace.

Chapter 10   What We Have Lost

"This is the way the world ends
Not with a bang but a whimper."

~ *T.S. Eliot*

December 21, 1983

With the 1982 calendar rollback, ANGSOC (American National Globalists – Supreme Overstate Command) is the ruling political party of the OverState. ANGSOC is unopposed. American National Globalists are neither Republican nor Democrat in their loyalties. They lean far to the left of any known party. All members, as socio-political elites, also are life members of the World Economic Forum and receive standing invitations to Davos and Bilderberg Group annual meetings, though now universally virtual.

The OverState rules with an iron fist through unilateral edict of the Deceiver in Chief, (DIC), who is the New Acirema WEFSOC. This title means he is the World Economic Fund Supreme Operating Commander. Each nation has one.

The WEFSOC heads of state are NOT capable leaders. They were selected by the globalist boards for their resemblance to sheep and because other sheep follow them. "Judas Sheep" they are called in the livestock industry, the one sheep that leads other sheep mindlessly to the slaughter.

The slaughter we've been led into is that we now live in a total surveillance state that is incapable of providing for its citizens, which roots out and crushes the slightest opposition. There is no longer a Constitution to protect citizens. We no longer have any rights, not even to life itself. These losses leave many with unbridled rage, especially the ones whose votes or candidates ushered in this living hell.

The OverState solution to pent up anger is provided daily with the help of the TechnoCrat arm of government, former entertainers, script writers and film experts.

In a unique experiment, guided scream therapy is presented in the privacy of one's home, though talk is that shuttered movie houses may soon be opened for the same purpose. The key to the guided scream therapy is The Scapegoat, an artificially created deep-fake face of hate.

One of the oddest constructs of the OverState, The Scapegoat is the brainchild of ANGSOC strategists to keep their constituents happy. TechnoCrats were tasked to create an expedient method for citizens to harmlessly vent their anger at their sorry state of affairs. Hence, The Scapegoat.

The Scapegoat is a dreary face and character, the official image on which to focus citizen anger and hate, rather than the OverState or one's fellow man.

Daily broadcasts permit citizens to scream their anger at those they blame for the New Normal within which we exist.

The scapegoat concept was hatched through research showing that ANGSOC were happier after watching media broadcast stories negative to conservatives. Most shouted or screamed at their telescreen during such programming, claiming relief from anxiety and depression symptoms in the process.

!!Trigger Warning!!

The actual person who inspired this bizarre ritual is said to be D.o.n.a.l.d T.r.u.m.p, the 45th President and likely the Last Republican President. (He has now gone into hiding and has not been heard from. If you notice, I used a simple method of lettering his name while still complying with the ban. Not because I am afraid of being seen, but so I do not betray my own thoughts. If anyone asks if I ever wrote "Donald Trump" in any media form, I can honestly say no).

Having been blamed for every form of racism and portrayed as "dangerous to our democracy", T.r.u.m.p's very name or image was said to create deep trauma and high anxiety for an entire generation of "snowflakes". The common name for this is T.r.u.m.p. Derangement Syndrome, or TDS.

Since it is now against the law to type, write or print his name or show any image of him due to widespread provocation of TDS symptoms, a substitute was needed, thus a scapegoat.

The Scapegoat image is an AI-created composite face of every objector in the global database, taken from ID's, surveillance video and facial recognition. AI even gave him the voice of a goat to go with the scapegoat concept. This face is displayed daily at the 800a morning broadcast, termed the Daily Hate. New Acirema starts the day, shouting, screaming.

The same ban is true for the former Founding Fathers. No one is allowed to publicly mention or discuss them. All national monuments, Jefferson, Lincoln, Washington, closed barricaded and draped over. All statues have been removed.

Part of my journey on public transport today has taken me along the former Monument Avenue. It seems strange to see the substantial marble pedestals rising up every block with no imposing bronze or marble figures astride their peaks.

Have I mentioned national travel has been suspended without receiving a prior permit? Such permits are only issued for work, and that must be connected with OverState roles and initiatives. Purpose must be proved even within the city.

Reflecting back, what we have lost is simply staggering. One day life was tooling along just fine for the average American, the citizen who lived in peaceful bliss of any efforts to subvert truth, justice and the American way. Then came August 11, 2021.

August 11, 2021 started as any normal day. FEMA and FCC had scheduled a joint Emergency Alert System test. Oddly and at the last minute, the UK and Australia moved to schedule their EAS tests that same day, international players joining our *national test*. Only the most obsessive news researchers knew about this in advance. I tried to tell people, to no avail.

By the end of that fateful day, FEMA and FCC had taken over the Internet and closed it to all communications, in an effort to prevent damage or intrusions to the Internet infrastructure. Similarly, all television and radio stations were shuttered, their permits yanked, and signals silenced, save for one.

That station, chosen for its loyalty to the OverState goals over the years and for affiliation with leading Hispanic broadcasters, was in for a surprise, including a name change. Leading liberal broadcasters were dumped in a broad purge, as were any entity, donors or property owners who strongly resisted the changes brought by the New Executive Orders.

The public, nearly driven to madness for two weeks without internet, social media, email, not even AM or FM radio broadcasts was hungry for programming. No newspapers or magazines were published during that two weeks. Some citizens, indeed some in the communications broadcast field, did not survive the outage, taking their lives in spite.

When word spread on the street that the broadcast signal would return every television screen worldwide was surrounded by a rapt audience.

The OverState signal did indeed resume at 2000p on August 25th, 2021. Two weeks of interim silence had allowed The OverState to conduct its activities in total media darkness.

Those activities included switching all televised OverState communications to a low-tech signal, black and white telecast. Wifi returned in a non-public format, limited to official use.

The first television broadcast began by declaring the Unified Date Change to 1982. Displayed in shockingly drab tones of some ancient low technology, with a choppy media edit of the infamous January 6 Capitol demonstration set to haunting, theatrical music, the template was cast for what is now a morning telecast known as the Daily Hate.

Against this backdrop, the Ten New Executive Orders were announced, with little explanation other than to say more information would be forth coming.

The featured "NWO Report" recorded the recent assassinations of the Haitian president and several African leaders during the first half of Old 2021. The 45th President and his Objector followers were implicated as the instigators of these horrific acts. Fake news returned in force that night.

The broadcast ended by calling for a Hate Night when all frustrations could be relieved, when all Objectors could be held accountable, when citizens were encouraged to call in to the FBI telethon style to report neighbors about whom one might have suspicions. Thus were the Snitches (females) and the Fedbois (males) born. Snitches and Fedbois, the equivalent of Hitler youth, will rat out their grandma for a few credits on their NBA, or for a narcotic session privilege token. To say families have been divided is a gross understatement.

As of August 25, 2021/1982, the period of Transition abruptly began. Within hours, the year had been rolled back to 1982, Congress was disbanded, all businesses were nationalized or closed. All military leaders were replaced with OverState members high in loyalty and low in morals. All news operations were converted to government property under CriPol enforcement and new locks.

The next broadcast came at 800a the following morning. The OverState labelled the broadcast "Values Unity Truth" but in fact the entire broadcast was dedicated to the notorious Scapegoat, the individual that supposedly precipitated our current precarious situation.

A list of The Scapegoat's failures, his missteps, complete with manufactured evidence regarding his treason charges was paraded across the screen in images and banners, though he had not been President for 7 months.

Traditional news times are gone, replaced with daily 800a and 2000p reports, now nothing more than propaganda, hyperbole and hate for The Scapegoat with overly optimistic reports related to the current Three-Year Plan for economic growth.

In every recorded instance of societal takeover, there are those elements of resistance, of defiance, that uncomfortably persist for long periods of time. I am proud to have documented several of these. When compliance to The OverState becomes equivalent with not existing at all, the motivation to give in to totalitarian demands erodes and soon evaporates. Those inclined to resist are left with no alternative but to rebel.

This is where I fit in, to document the Objector resistance by blending into their settings to feed information back to the OverState. That is how it works, in theory.

Although life has been tough, and is getting worse, I don't want to leave you with a hopeless, totally dark scenario. There are bright spots of kindness that remind one of how things were. I think our state of mind comes down to our beliefs.

While not a religious man, I frequently recall snippets of verses and songs voiced by my mother, before we lost her. She was bright, and happy, and loved her family, and the Bible. She often reminded me that God is with us through anything, if we but believe. My faith in her words and guidance grows with each passing day.

My thoughts are with those who have lost the most in these changes. Those of us who have lived, at least a little, are not the worst off. Nor are the formerly rich, although they have lost the most.

The little ones of the cities, our children, have suffered the most and will continue to do so. Frightened, penned in, seldom allowed to play, vaxx-pin-cushions, their lives are shaped by the OverState in every mode of entertainment that other children have traditionally enjoyed. By movies, games, books, school, even by playtimes.

It is for these that my heart grieves the deepest. For in my visits to the Objector zones, I have seen their children at play, in fresh air, enjoying themselves. Laughing.

I never hear laughter inside the city limits.

Chapter 11 The Rise of New Acirema

"A nation that forgets its past has no future".
~Winston Churchill

December 21, 1983

NEO-010 was the final NEO signed, sealing the upheaval forced upon us. NEO-010 dictated the immediate replacement of every mention of America with the name New Acirema.

Acirema is simply America written backwards, a name symbolizing the staggering upheaval and turmoil that has been going on since 1982, the final insult to a battered nation.

NEO-010 declared New Acirema into existence as a geographical District conforming to the North American continent including all of Canada and Mexico.

The name New Acirema is part of the 1982 Transition, to be confirmed at the end of the 1983 Consolidation. Names and terms must be voted on by The OverState and confirmed by WEFCOM in London by January 1, 1984 to be considered permanent.

The name change for the nation was enacted for several reasons according to The OverState broadcast. The first was to remove any indication of America in its uniqueness and former greatness. The term "America First" has been outlawed for public or private usage.

Another reason that has been given is the "triggering" effect that the name America has had on the mental health of an entire generation of snowflake, thin-skinned citizens.

The real reason for the name change, we all know, is due to COGB. China Our Gracious Benefactor. Few people know that pre-1982, China was the largest purchaser of American Treasury bonds. They owned us through our debt. Our debt interest had become unsustainable, in the trillions of dollars.

For years China sold us cheap and plentiful goods created with slave and near-slave labor, then used our own money to invest in our debt. Our bankrupt treasury lapped up their money, but our nation was left beholden to them once the economy crashed in August 1982.

A huge component of the Great Reset was the resetting of our debt with China. That reset did not come without onerous obligations.

China became a vocal opponent to the name America. The OverState needed their help to rebuild our lagging infrastructure. So Chinese partnerships were formed for transportation, highways and housing projects. China Our Gracious Benefactor, as they insist on being called, won with the help of the Deceiver in Chief, the DIC leading our nation.

In NEO-010, the U.S. flag was changed as well. The addition of two more states, first Washington, D. C., then Puerto Rico gave reason for this change, but the real momentum behind the change was the staggering opposition to all things American, history, symbols, documents. The U.S. Constitution, as unique a document as has ever been written at the founding of a nation, has been suspended, along with the Bill of Rights. Suspended is the term used, rather than voided, a softer approach to a very sticky wicket. Of course, the Declaration of Independence has likewise been scrubbed from public view or distribution. We hear that ANGSOC is writing a new document, loosely termed "The Denial of Independence".

All evidence of America as it was has been erased. Monuments gone, flag gone, history rewritten.

The unconfirmed word is that these changes have happened on a similar timetable world-wide. Without the internet or even telephones, we have no international communication. Little word makes its way across the oceans.

Acirema is a very isolated nation-state, save for membership in WEFCOM and its partnership with COGB, China Our Gracious Benefactor.

Chapter 12 In Closing

December 21, 1983

I am still aboard the public transport at this point. My fellow riders are very few now, mostly miners, a few others headed for the Fishing Platforms on the return loop. One passenger suddenly died and was removed at the last stop.

The air is stale and thick, making it a struggle to breathe. The strongest odors are the tarry smell of coal dust and old sweat. A drift of pot vapor makes its way forward now and again. I draw air in slowly through my face shield and fight the urge to cough.

I skipped my appointment at the Benefits Center. I impulsively decided to forego that stop because I can no longer avoid being processed for my new ID implant. This decision will cause me some difficulty in purchasing goods, but since most commercial exchange has turned to barter, I believe I can manage. I can still transfer credits, for now.

Speaking of barter, I did mention that it has become commonplace to exchange sex for goods and services? Still amazes me. On this transport, as one example, I have been openly propositioned three times in less than two hours.

This form of currency has reached such proportions as to generate talk from The OverState of the formation of an Anti-Sex League, for lack of a better term, that purportedly promotes chastity but in actuality has as its goal the stabilization of commerce, to interrupt this form of barter.

Since there is no paper or metal currency, pods of laundry detergent or shower soap have become hot mediums of exchange, given their limited supply and distribution.

I am still several kilometers from the point of origin for the bus lines, the point where they are charged, but obviously never cleaned. Yes, kilometers is the term I intended. Under WEFCOM the metric system has been globally imposed. This impacts Nacirema the hardest.

The next stop will be where the miners change from transport to train to go to work. Those headed to the coast for the Fishing Platforms will remain on board.

Coal is still mined in our district for export, though it is not permitted to be used for any purpose inside New Acirema. The miners will transfer to the new MagLev trains installed by, and in a station built by COGB, China Our Gracious Benefactor. China gets the coal. We are its coal mine.

At top speeds of 370 MPH, the miners will travel hundreds of miles in less than 30 minutes. That's less commute time than the time it takes to hear the latest OverState economic statistics announced subliminally beneath the whine of the high-speed train.

You may have ventured a guess that I harbor certain secrets, secrets that could have me transferred to the Walgag, those former big-box shopping areas now converted to detention facilities. (Some are even rumored to house mass morgues. I'm not going close enough to find out.)

Corporations that cooperated with The OverState receive workers to create the products that they formerly imported from around the world. Only resources are imported now. The workers are forced to live at these facilities, work there, finding themselves essentially imprisoned.

The gulags, or Walgags, are the new lockup of the "Objectors" who argued and fought so vehemently and valiantly to expose the gross invalidity of the most recent presidential elections. They were racked and hunted through the TPI program, the *Think Police,* which is purported to investigate one's very intentions.

From my investigative reporting, I know some things that I shouldn't. I'm relieved no one is running the TPI program to investigate *my* intentions. At least I hope they are not.

For instance, *I would not want* TPI to know my thoughts regarding a certain unconfiscated vehicle, sitting on blocks in a barn on my remote family farm. Or that I know where extra fuel barrels are buried. Or that I know that until recently the vehicle has been started and maintained.

It is a 1996 Jeep Cherokee, lifted, with a brush guard. My father left it to me. He bought it, with a salvage title, garaged it for repairs and rebuilt it. He never titled the vehicle in his name. I have only seen it in a single foto. I have the foto in my boot. I only look at the foto when I am certain that it is safe.

This vehicle calls to me. Or is it the freedom that such a vehicle represents? I'm finding that call hard to resist. Dare I make a run for it?

This Jeep has a powerful engine, is painted flat black and treated on all glass and chrome for minimum light reflectivity. It has weapons installed, my father's note read. In the grill, the ceilings, consoles, and floor. To hunt, he said. Not that I have ever owned or used weapons, but I can learn. It has railroad timber bumpers and no-flat tires. The intriguing part is the obstacle chutes, consisting of interior fender canisters of golf balls and nail clusters designed to disrupt pursuing vehicles.

The farm itself is on a high wooded bluff that overlooks a river. I remember going there as a boy, the million stone steps down to the river, where a sturdy boat house held a wooden sailboat above the water in a sling.

I'm telling you these things in confidence. Don't betray my trust. My uncle cautioned a few letters back that we must be concerned with any who style themselves as our friends as much as the Wildmen and the bandits. Our friends, he says, are to be suspected above all others. They know what is to be gained from us, where a complete stranger can only guess. It is a dismal view, but I have no one else to rely on. For as long as we can remain in contact, I will trust my Uncle Winston as my main source of advice as well as wisdom. After that, I will be on my own.

My uncle is, after all, a survivor. Winston learned early on to watch his back, to keep his opinions to himself, blend in and survive.

Winston's beloved Britain fell to the global changes long before America did, so long ago that Britain is now the seat of the WEFCOM NWO. I hate that about Britain. I also hate that my father was killed there more than a year ago.

As the elder brother, my father felt compelled to visit his only sibling before travel was completely shut down. Uncle Winston had finally seen a doctor after a year. Just a cough he said. Turned out to be early-stage tuberculosis, just as feared. After a few brief, burdened days my father prepared to return.

My father died on that visit to London, October of 1982. 13 months ago. That's why I don't talk about him. The victim of a raging mob protesting "racially motivated lockdowns", he was burned alive in his car. I despise his killers and the whole affair. I am not opposed to free speech or assembly. I am opposed to blocking a man's car doors to burn him to death.

A naturalized American, but no less American than myself and grateful for his political and economic freedoms, my father had long been called a conservative, then later labeled a Republican. The truth was that he was neither.

Larger than life, my father was a man too big for any labels to fit. In truth he was his own man, tolerating no other rule. He truly felt he had declared his independence by migrating to America, yet found himself, in the end, being branded an Objector due to his resistance to domestic pandemic mandates of The OverState and by his mere presence driving near a BLM rally. Silver lining? The reputation that he established has become my "in" to research the Objector resistance.

I regret that I did not receive his ashes. Now I have no permanent address to receive them. The only personal things of his I have at all fit in one small black duffel, currently resting behind my back, slung across my shoulder beneath my winter jacket. I inherited other things. They just aren't here, in the city.

As I closed up Father's apartment prior to being evicted, I found one letter from him taped onto an old wooden cigar box, along with a duffel bag of goods. Both were labeled simply. "Open in Event of Emergency."

If this isn't an emergency, I don't know what is.

I am not without options. I could stay and fight, but I have no supplies, no platform. Single players such as myself have no standing and are therefore powerless. I keep telling myself I can make my own way, as if saying it will make it happen.

I know that I cannot bend to the will of those who are ruling. The OverState and I share nothing in common.

I have a hand drawn map to my father's land, my only other possession bearing his long, scrawled hand. I can make my own way, the further from the cities, the better. Fewer cameras, fewer microphones, fewer Snitches and Fedbois. Fewer CriPols or Think Police. Every man for himself, so to speak. Though I do wish I could have a dog.

I have in my day bag a miner coverall and helmet. I obtained these from a bench near the confiscation yard bus collection point. Still wrapped in the plastic. Someone who realized they could not tolerate the mines, or perhaps never made it there to begin with.

There are less than a dozen riders on the bus now. One woman about my age caught my eye. I doubt she's here to solicit. She looks too young to be a miner, but her hands and nails show grime, as if she is a mechanic. She wears the loose blue coverall of a miner. The bulge in her backpack screams helmet. Her wristband tells me that she has been able to avoid the vaxx so far. It is the same color as mine, issued by a former newspaper publisher. No visible necrotic scars.

She moves to sit beside me.

I offer her a small bar of chocolate, a Yank custom from WWII, universally known for making friends. It is one I have been saving. Somehow it has managed to not melt.

She accepts.

If she is on this transport, she works the late shift. No private travel is authorized at this hour, so she must be headed to the mines, like me.

I stand up, joints stiff, swaying as I remove my jacket and the black duffel. I struggle into the coveralls after noisily unwrapping their sterile cover.

"First day on the job?" she asks.

"Better than the newspaper plant," I smile.

She glances at her grubby nails. She knows that I know her secret.

"You should hurry," she points, directing my attention to the transfer station looming ahead. It is dully lit, with the weak, washed-out look of CFL lighting. It is snowing now.

I look into her eyes, then to her shoulders. I notice that she is not wearing any affiliation pins. Another good sign.

I finish dressing, then sling the duffel over my shoulder, covering it with my coat. I remain standing.

"Since it's your first night, follow me," she said, standing up. A beeping countdown commenced, signaling the remaining seconds to disembark the transport.

"I will show you where to go, what to do, if you like."

"I'm grateful," I said, a bit suspiciously. As we pulled up to the station, I looked back toward the glow of the city just as final curfew struck, dimming all but a few ominous strobe lights. I would rather die than to submit my future to the crushing rule of The OverState.

"There's nothing for us there," she said in a calm voice, looking straight ahead. "The future is out there."

"My name is Winton," I volunteered, easing my tone.

"I am Tara," the woman whispered. "Let's go."

It was, in that moment, that I decided my entire future.

I will go with Tara. We will somehow escape this train. I will find my family farm, the Jeep, the freedom. I will escape New Acirema. I will find America. This is my goal, or I will die trying. For the first time in years, I feel no fear.

I feel destined to become, as was my father before me, an Objector. My confidence in taking this direction is strong.

Take heart and take heed. Liberty will prevail once more, if we are diligent and persist in our struggle.

This is, by no means, the end.

Appendices

The New Dictionary – Selected terms

New Acirema	Transitional name for America
ANGSOC	Acirema National Globalists-Supreme OverState Command Ruling Party of the OverState
Citizens	Residents of New Acirema
Deceiver in Chief	World Economic Fund Strategic Organization Chairman. Also DIC.
DoubleSpeak	Remedial Language of the Word-Smiths
EVP	Enhanced Vaxx Protocol- monthly citizen vaxxination protocol, 8 Vaxxes Total
NBA	Needs Based Allowance
Objectors	Former citizens opposed to 2020 election results, vaxx mandates; considered enemies of the OverState
OverState	Ruling government body, Combined Executive, Judicial and Technocratic branches of Acirema government
Privileges	Access to former basics: Showers, Hot water, Privacy
The Scapegoat	AI avatar construct for release of pent-up anger & hate, using deep fake technology.

Technocratic	Socio-technical government arm "Guiding Society Thru Hi-Tech"
VaxxPass	Combined ID/Travel/Vaxx document
Walgag	Big Box retail locations now used as gulag detainment and BPCs
WEFCOM	World Economic Fund Command, based in London.
WEFSOC	World Economic Fund Supreme OverState Chairman. One per District. See also DIC

Key Dates and Timeline

July 5th, 2021

Executive Orders 001 thru 010 written
Major distracting events including
-Collapsing Infrastructure Buildings and Bridges
-Assassinations of prominent world figures, Presidents
-Cuban, South African, French, Haitian Revolutions

August 11, 2021

-Joint FCC and FEMA Emergency Alert System test over both radio and wifi warning systems "goes awry", resulting in blocked radio broadcast and internet connections worldwide.
-Military leaders quietly purged and held on base arrest.
-Congress disbanded but not permitted to leave their respective House and Senate buildings until August 25 to control information leaks.

August 25, 2021 becomes August 25, 1982

-The Ten New Executive Orders (NEOs) signed & enacted
-Calendar Year Changed by Executive Order - 2021 to 1982
-All Churches Shuttered, Doors Blocked or Welded Shut
-Constitution and Bill of Rights suspended
-Grocery stores, and distribution networks nationalized.
-Fossil fuels (gas, oil, coal) nationalized.
-Newspapers nationalized.
-Journalists conscripted into OverState service.

-January 1, 2022 reset to January 1, 1983.
-The Year of Consolidation
-January 1, 2023 reset to January 1, 1984.

From the Author

"1982: A Prequel to Orwell's 1984" was written as a fanfiction homage.

It was also written as a warning, for those who will listen.

You may question this timeline of events. You should. Always question what you are told, use your intelligence, conduct research. Astute Analysis begins with a Question.

Test opinions, evaluate results, draw conclusions. Just ensure that they are your own conclusions.

Do not rely on the judgement of others when it comes to your life, your future and your family's well-being.

While everything we are told is for *someone's* benefit, not everything we are told is for *our* benefit.

I have enjoyed conducting the research for this novel and trust that you will search out the terms and concepts on your own. This is so important to you, the reader, reaching your own conclusions on matters of importance.

Thank you for your purchase.

About the Author

In addition to this novel, Malcom Massey writes "The Martin Culver Series", a series of action thrillers based on his experiences living in Central and South America, as well as his interests in history, archaeology and travel. The main character of the series, Martin Culver, is an author-turned-adventurer who gets unavoidably drawn into one dangerous exploit after another.

Culver's passion to repatriate stolen historical artifacts leads him to establish the International Antiquities Foundation (IAF), but the archaeological black market has deep roots, with shadowy players on both sides of the fence, players who do not abide any interference and who play for keeps. As Culver builds his team of IAF experts, knowing who to trust is the first lesson he must learn. The lessons that follow will test every fiber of his character.

The Martin Culver Series is best for the reader when read in order.

Malcom grew up devouring stories of ancient cultures and lost treasures from around the world. Raised in Virginia, Malcom has lived in Costa Rica and Bolivia, and has traveled throughout South America and the Caribbean, including Peru, Ecuador, Mexico, the Bahamas, the Dominican Republic and the Virgin Islands.

After living and writing for 16 months in the Yucatan Peninsula, Malcom returned to the United States, where he still lives and writes near the coast.

Links
Author Blog
www.malcommassey.com

Amazon Author Website
www.amazon.com/author/malcommassey

Made in the USA
Las Vegas, NV
18 December 2023

83085263R00046